To Mikie - Charlie - Sam
+ Mary

Love -
Grandma
& Granddad T.

Jan. 1989

My Big BEDTIME BOOK

© This edition, Ward Lock Limited 1988

This 1988 edition published by Derrydale Books,
distributed by Crown Publishers, Inc.,
225 Park Avenue South, New York, New York 10003

ISBN 0–517–66809–2

h g f e d c b a

Printed and bound in Czechoslovakia

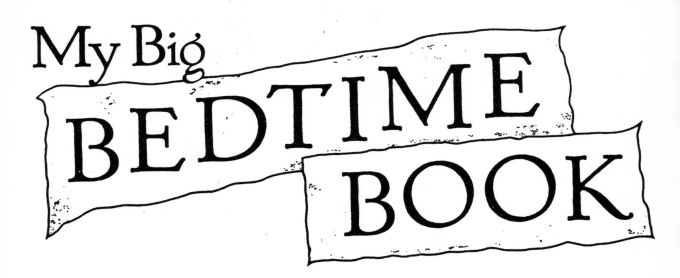

My Big BEDTIME BOOK

Illustrated by H.G.C. Marsh Lambert

DERRYDALE BOOKS
NEW YORK

RING-A-RING O' ROSES

R ING-A-RING o' roses,
  A pocket full of posies,—

A-tish-oo, a-tish-oo,
  We all fall down !

5

1
2
One,
Two,
Buckle
My
Shoe,

Three,
Four,
Knock
at the
Door,

3
4

5
6
Five,
Six,
Pick up
Sticks,

7
8
Seven,
Eight,
Lay
Them
Straight,

9
Nine,
Ten,
A Good
Fat
Hen.
10

1 2 3 4 5 6 7 8 9 0

JANUARY

Frost upon the windows,
Snow upon the trees,
Ice upon the puddles,
—**How** my hands do freeze!

Aches in all my fingers,
Chilblains on my toes.
Sitting by the fire, I
Rub my crimson
nose.

In comes dear old
Nannie—
" What are you
about ?
Put your wool-
lies on, child,
You are
going out ! "

Out of doors and running
    Soon I'm in a glow.
Fires are very nice, but—
    Nurse knows best, you know!

DO WHAT YOU'RE TOLD

Do what you're told,
Come when you're bid,
Shut the door after you,
Never be chid.

I'LL SING YOU A SONG

I'LL sing you a song—
  Though not very long,
Yet I think it as pretty as any;
      Put your hand in your
        purse,
      You'll never be worse,
      And give the poor singer
        a penny.

AS I WAS GOING TO SELL MY EGGS

AS I was going to sell my eggs,
   I met a man with bandy legs,
Bandy legs and crooked toes,
I tripped up his heels, and he fell on his nose.

HE THAT WOULD THRIVE

HE that would thrive
   Must rise at five;
He that hath thriven
May lie till seven;
And he that by the plough would thrive,
Himself must either hold or drive.

BABY BUNTING'S VISIT TO TOY TOWN

The moonlight was streaming into the room, and it was ever so late, but somehow Baby Bunting couldn't go to sleep.

"Would you like to come to Toy Town with me?" asked a soft voice.

Baby Bunting sat up. It was Teddy Bear speaking.

"I'd **love** it," said Baby Bunt- ing.

So Teddy Bear led Baby Bunting to the window-sill. They sat down together on an extra strong moon-beam, and soon the fairies had drawn them right up to Toy Town, which, Baby Bunting learnt, is in the heart of Cloudland.

How Baby Bunting loved it all!

The houses were made of wood and painted brightly, and busy doll people were running about everywhere.

Here was a baker's shop, where Mrs. Dutchie handed cakes and buns over

the counter to the Toy Folk, and just over the way stood a greengrocer's stall.

"There is a market on," said Teddy. "That is why we are meeting so many animals."

As he spoke Mr. Noah passed, driving a great herd of cows and sheep.

"That is where Peter Rabbit lives," said Teddy, pointing to a bright yellow house, " and the green and red one next to it is mine. Come along." And with a

tiny latch-key he opened the door and welcomed Baby Bunting inside.

"Do you come here every night when I'm asleep?" asked Baby Bunting.

"Generally," answered Teddy. "Now I want to take you round the garden."

It was such a pretty little garden, full of flowers, and with a well in the middle.

Baby Bunting peered over the edge of the well and down into the clear water.

And then—suddenly— Splash!

Baby Bunting had tumbled in!

"Where am I?" asked Baby Bunting sleepily.

"Time to get up," said Mummie's well-known voice. "Wake up, pet. Look—all your toys are wide awake and Teddy is having a dance on the floor!"

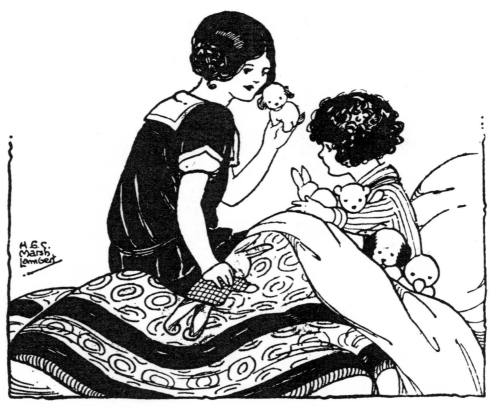

So Baby Bunting got up.

Now I wonder if that visit to Toy Town was all a dream, after all?

I rather think it must have been!

This is a dream. Baby Bunting knows
not to play near water when she is awake.
It is dangerous.

BLIND MAN'S BUFF

"If I **only** could see you," poor
Timothy cries,
" But I can't, with this bandage right
over my eyes!"

19

The Balloon Race

It is by me.

Ah! It is up.

I am up
by it.

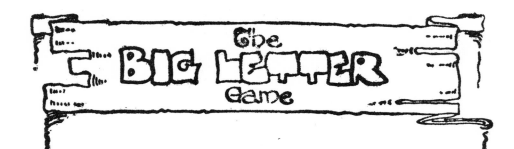

The BIG LETTER Game

Which is the **A**
in this little word
ALL ?

Which is the **B** in

this big

bounce-y

BALL ?

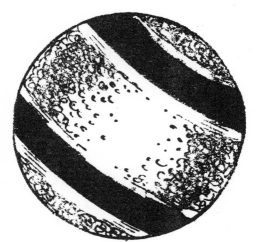

Which is the C in this
BRICK made of
wood?

Which is the D
in this
MAIDEN
so good?

Which is the **E** in this pretty green **LEAF**?

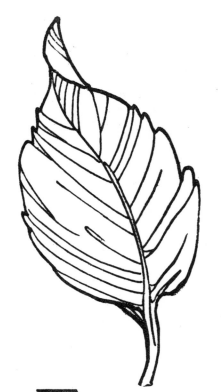

Which is the **F** in this nice joint of **BEEF?**

Which is the
G in this
DOG on
the mat?

Which is the
H in this
little
boy's
HAT?

Which is the I
in this
CHILD
by the sea?

Which is the J in
this
JELLY
for me

Which is the
K in this
small dolly's
SOCK?

Which is the L
in the
SILK
of this
frock?

A frock is a dress — did you know?

Which is the M in this MAT on the floor?

Which is the N in the KNOB of this door?

Which is the O in this long curly ROPE?

Which is the P in this nice cake of SOAP?

Which is the Q in this QUEEN on her throne?

Which is the R in this GIRL all alone?

Which is the S in this little bird's NEST?

Which is the T in this old wooden CHEST?

Which is the U in this MOUSE by its hole?

Which is the V in this VAN full of coal?

Which is the W in this WATCH made of gold?

Which is the X in this FOX with a cold?

Which is the Y in this little girl's TOY?

Which is the Z in the PRIZE for this boy?

THE WONDER BOOK

W
ASHING DAY

ORANGES & LEMONS

Oranges and lemons,
Say the bells of St. Clement's.
You owe me five farthings,
Say the bells of St. Martin's.

When will you pay me?
Say the bells of Old Bailey.
When I grow rich,
Say the bells of Shoreditch.

How many rabbits can you see?

If I were an apple
And grew upon a tree,
I think I'd fall down
On a nice boy like me.
I wouldn't stay there,
Giving nobody joy;
I'd fall down at once,
And say, "Eat me, my boy!"

DICK'S DAYS AT THE FARM.

WHEN Dick was getting better after whooping cough, Mummy made a most lovely plan!—and when it was all settled, she told Dick about it.

And what do you think it was?

He was to spend a whole fortnight on a farm down in Somerset!

. . . . . .

Dick had always loved animals, so when, on his first morning in the country,

40

Farmer Evans asked him, with a twinkle in his eye, if he would like to see his "family," Dick knew at once that he was going to take him round the farm, and he jumped with joy.

What a lot of animals there were, too!

First they went to see the pigs, and Dick was allowed to give old Mrs. Tompkins, the Tamworth sow, a bucketful of potato parings. How she loved them, and oh what a noise she made as she ate them!   Her manners weren't a bit polite!

"Come along, Dick," laughed Farmer Evans. "Now here we are at the shed where our youngest calf is. You would like to see him, wouldn't you?   He is only two days old, and lives in here with Daisy, his mother."

Dick peeped in at the pretty brown and white calf, and then the farmer took him to see the sheep and lambs.   One of the lambs was quite tame, and let Dick give him some milk in a bottle.

After that, the farmer showed Dick ever so many more interesting things. He saw the horses and the dogs, and the cows, including the beautiful Prize Shorthorn, and two gentle Alderneys.

"You must get up early to-morrow," said the farmer, "and then you will be able to watch the cows being milked."

"Can I milk one?" asked Dick.

"It's not very easy at first," answered the farmer, "but you can try to learn, if you like. Martha, the dairymaid, will teach you to milk one of the goats—we have three or four nanny-goats, you know, and then after that, perhaps you may be able to milk a cow."

And Dick was so eager to learn that long before his fortnight was up he had learnt to milk Marigold, one of the Alderneys, all by himself.

He learnt how to skim the milk, too, and how to make Devonshire, or clotted, cream, and how to make butter, and cream cheese, and oh! how he

enjoyed his time on the farm.

When at last the holiday was over, Dick felt quite sad, and as he leant out of the train to say good-bye to kind Farmer Evans, he whispered:

"If—if any of the men get ill, or you need any extra help—you will send for me, won't you?"

"Aye, that I will!" said Farmer Evans, heartily, and he waved his red and green handkerchief till the train was quite out of sight.

What are the names of the
big and little **black** letters
on this page?

Dance, little **b**a**b**y, dance up **high** ;

Never **m**ind, baby, mother **is** nigh.

Crow and ca**p**er, caper and cro**w**.

There, little baby, there **you** go !

Up **t**o the **c**eiling, down to the

ground,

Bac**kw**ar**d**s and **f**orwards, round

and ro**un**d,

So dance little **b**aby, mother will sing,

With the merry caro**l**—

ding, ding, di**n**g !

JACK AND JILL

JACK and Jill went up the hill
   To fetch a pail of water ;
Jack fell down and cracked his crown,
And Jill came tumbling after.

Then up Jack got, and home did trot,
As fast as he could caper,
They put him to bed and plaster'd his
   head
With vinegar and brown paper.

A FROG HE WOULD
A-WOOING GO

A FROG he would a-wooing go,
    Heigho! says Rowley,
Whether his mother would let him or no.
    With a rowley, powley, gammon and
        spinach,
    Heigho! says Anthony Rowley.

So off he set with his opera hat,
    Heigho! says Rowley,
And on the way he met with a Rat.
    With a rowley, powley, gammon and
        spinach,
    Heigho! says Anthony Rowley.

"Now pray, Mr. Rat, won't you come with
me,"
Heigho! says Rowley,
"Kind Mrs. Mousey for to see?"
With a rowley, powley, gammon and
spinach,
Heigho! says Anthony Rowley.

"Pray, Mrs. Mouse, are you within?"
Heigho! says Rowley,
"Yes, kind sirs, I'm sitting to spin."
With a rowley, powley, gammon and
spinach,
Heigho! says Anthony Rowley.

But while they were all a merry-making,
Heigho! says Rowley,
A cat and her kittens came tumbling in.
With a rowley, powley, gammon and
spinach,
Heigho! says Anthony Rowley.

The cat she seized the rat by the crown;
Heigho! says Rowley,
And the kittens pulled the little mouse down.
With a rowley, powley, gammon and
spinach,
Heigho! says Anthony Rowley.

This put Mr. Frog in a terrible fright,
  Heigho! says Rowley,
He put on his hat, and he wished them good-
    night.
    With a rowley, powley, gammon and
      spinach,
    Heigho! says Anthony Rowley.

ST. SWITHIN'S DAY

ST. Swithin's Day, if thou dost rain,
  For forty days it will remain:
St. Swithin's Day, if thou be fair,
For forty days 'twill rain na mair.

PUSSY-CAT, PUSSY-CAT

PUSSY-CAT, pussy-cat, where have you
    been?
I've been to London to see the Queen.
Pussy-cat, pussy-cat, what did you there?
I caught a little mouse under her chair.

The Man in
the Moon
looked out of
the Moon,
And this is what he
said—

"It's time,
now
that I'm
getting
up,
All Babies
were
in Bed!"

FAIRY DAYS.

THE fairies often came to me
    When I was very small.
I hardly ever see them now
    That I am growing tall;
And when I'm quite grown up, I know
    They'll never come at all!

There's lots of things I'll like to do
    When I'm grown up, I know—
The things I've never been allowed

THE FAIRIES

Who are you?

To do before.　And so
I sometimes wish I could be quick
　　And grow and grow and grow!
But only sometimes!　Then I think
　　Of what will have to be—
How never more the Fairy Folk
　　Will come and talk to me.
And oh, it hurts!　It hurts because
　　I love them so, you see.

SING A SONG OF SIXPENCE

SING a Song of Sixpence,
   A pocket full of rye;
Four-and-twenty blackbirds
   Baked in a pie

When the pie was opened,
   The birds began to sing;

Was not that a dainty
dish
   To set before the
   King?

The King was in the counting-house,

Counting out his money;

The Queen was in the parlour,
Eating bread and honey;

The maid was in the garden,
Hanging out the clothes;

When down came a little bird

And snapped off her nose!

LEG OVER LEG

LEG over leg,
    As the dog went to Dover;
When he came to a stile
Hop! he went over.

DOCTOR FOSTER WENT TO GLOSTER

DOCTOR Foster went to Gloster,
    In a shower of rain;
He stepped in a puddle, up to the middle,
And never went there again.

MATILDA MIRANDA McKANE.

MATILDA Miranda McKane,
Why are you so silly
    and vain?
    You spend hours at the glass,
    Though it tells you, alas,
That you're really exceedingly plain.

Matilda Miranda McKane,
You have eaten ten buns in the train—
    You are feeling quite seedy?
    Of course.   You're so greedy.
And I hope that you will have a pain.

Matilda Miranda McKane.
You have walked for five
    miles in the rain.
In the thinnest of frocks,
And without shoes or
    socks.
I really don't think you are sane.

Matilda Miranda McKane,
Your uncleanliness causes me pain.
Do you ever use soap?
To be candid, I hope
That I never shall meet you again.

SOAP BUBBLES.

SOAP BUBBLES

When I've lots of little troubles,

Then I like to watch the bubbles

Go a-sailing and a-sailing,

To and fro.

For the bubbles that I'm making,

Soon, I know, will be a-breaking

◇ ◇ ◇ ◇ ◇

And my troubles, like the bubbles,

All will go!

JACK, BE NIMBLE

JACK, be nimble,
  Jack, be quick,
And Jack, jump over the
  candlestick.

PETER, PETER, PUMPKIN EATER

PETER, Peter, pumpkin eater
  Had a wife and couldn't keep her;
He put her in a pumpkin shell,
And there he kept her very well.

Peter, Peter, pumpkin eater,
Had another, but didn't love her.
Peter learnt to read and spell
And then he loved her very well.

THE THREE BEARS

ONE day a little girl, whose name was Goldilocks, went out for a walk before break-fast. She found a dear little cot-tage near a wood, and as the door was open she went inside.

She found a big bowl, and a mid-dle sized bowl, and a ti-ny bowl, full of por-ridge, and she

tried them all in turn, but she only liked the por-ridge in the ti-ny bowl, and **that** she ate right up.

Then she saw a big chair, and a mid-dle sized chair, and a ti-ny chair, but she did not find the two bigger ones at all comfy, so she sat down ve-ry hard in the ti-ny chair—so hard, that she broke the seat of it!

Then she went up-stairs and found

a big bed, and a mid-dle sized bed, and a ti-ny bed, and the ti-ny bed was so comfy that she went fast asleep in it.

Now that cot-tage be-longed to three bears, and by-and-by they came home.

"Who has been eating **my** por-ridge?" said the big Dad-dy Bear, and "Who has been eating **mine**?" said the mid-dle sized Mum-my Bear,

and "Oh dear, somebody's eaten **my** por-ridge **all** up!" squeaked the ti-ny Baby Bear.

Then the bears saw that somebody had been sit-ting in their chairs, too, and oh dear!—they **were** so cross! "**My** chair is broken," cried Baby Bear—"Who **can** have done it?"

Then the bears went upstairs, and when they found Goldilocks fast asleep in Baby Bear's bed, they made such

a noise that the little girl woke up! She was so frightened when she saw the bears that she rolled off the bed ever so quickly, and ran down-stairs and out of the cot-tage before the bears could stop her. And she ran and she ran until she got home safely to her Mum-my.

Well, Goldilocks got home that night
Quite scared! I think it served her right.
But in the morning, feeling better,
She wrote a friendly little letter
To Mummy Bear, and asked if they
Would come to tea with her that day.
And then she set to work to make
A very special plummy cake.

MULTIPLICATION IS VEXATION

MULTIPLICATION is vexation,
Division is as bad:
The Rule of Three doth puzzle me,
And Spelling drives me mad.

SOLOMON GRUNDY

SOLOMON GRUNDY,
    Born on a Monday,
Christened on Tuesday,
Married on Wednesday,
Took ill on Thursday,
Worse on Friday,
Died on Saturday,
Buried on Sunday:
That was the end
Of Solomon Grundy.

OH, THAT I WAS WHERE I WOULD BE!

OH, that I was where I
    would be,
Then would I be where I am
    not!
But where I am I must be,
And where I would be I
    cannot.

LITTLE BO-PEEP

LITTLE Bo-peep has lost her sheep
   And can't tell where to find them;
Leave them alone and they'll come home
   And bring their tails behind them.

Little Bo-peep fell fast asleep
   And dreamt she heard them bleating;
But when she awoke, she found it a joke,
   For they were still a-fleeting.

Then up she took her little crook,
   Determined for to find them;
She found them indeed, but it made her
     heart bleed,
   For they'd left their tails behind
     them.

HEY, DIDDLE, DIDDLE

HEY, diddle, diddle, the cat and the
    fiddle,
   The cow jumped over the moon;
The little dog laughed to see such sport,
   While the dish ran away with the
    spoon.

LITTLE BO-PEEP.

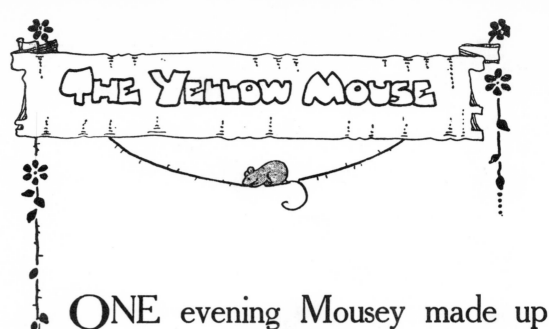

THE YELLOW MOUSE

ONE evening Mousey made up his mind to leave his home and see the world. His world was the nursery, where just now all was dark and quiet, except for the flicker and glow of the fire in the grate. His home was a warm and cosy nest right under the boards, which his mother had made for him and his brothers.

But Mousey was tired of the nest, and when Mrs. Mouse had left her children to look for her supper he slipped out after her, and ran up the dark passage to the world above.

He was a pretty little thing. His toes were pink and so was the tip of his nose. His coat was soft and brown and furry and his eyes shone like big black beads. His tail was a wonder, so long and so slender.

Scrit-scratch went his tiny feet on the nursery floor as he ran. "What a lot of strange smells!" thought Mousey. He sniffed first round the coal-box, and then near the cat's basket, and then under the table, where some cake-crumbs had fallen. The last smell made him so curious that he tasted a crumb with his little pink tongue, and then for the next few minutes he was busy. Nibble, nibble, one crumb after another, till he had had a good supper.

Soon Mousey found himself at the foot of the table-leg. "This goes up," said he, "and so will I." He stuck

his sharp claws into the wood, and up he went. The table-cloth, too, was a help, for he could stick his claws into that.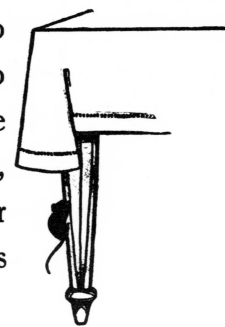

At last he was up, and there was a great surprise for Mousey. For in the middle stood a strange little house shut in by bars that shone like gold in the fire-light. Behind the golden bars sat a golden prisoner. "Hurrah!" cried Mousey, in his thin squeak, "this must be the yellow mouse my mother

has told me of.   It is he who sings so loudly in the sunshine when we brown mice are hiding away.   I will set him free and take him home and he shall teach us to sing loudly too."

Mousey gripped the golden bars with his tiny sharp teeth, and bit hard and fast.   "Twing, twang," said the bars, and the golden prisoner woke. He ruffled his feathers and gave an angry squawk.   "Ugly little brown mouse, what are you doing here? **Squawk! Squawk!**"

Timid Mousey gave one look at him as he flew, beating his wings round his

cage, and then rushed to the edge of the table. Down by the cloth he swung and scrit-scratched across the floor. He did not stop till he was safe in his cosy dark nest again.

SWINGING.

Up where the birdies fly,
Swinging, singing, oh so high.
Down where the daisies grow,
Swinging, singing, oh so low.

HOT CROSS BUNS

HOT cross buns! hot cross buns!
    One a penny, two a penny,
Hot cross buns!

If you have no daughters
Give them to your sons;
One a penny, two a penny
Hot cross buns.

DUNCE, DUNCE, DOUBLE D

DUNCE, dunce, double D,
    Could not learn his A.B.C.;
Put the cap on, then you'll see,
What a stupid boy is he!
Dunce, dunce, double D.

LITTLE JACK HORNER

LITTLE Jack Horner
    Sat in a corner,
Eating a Christmas pie;
He put in his thumb,
And pulled out a plum,
And cried, "What a good boy am I!"

TWEEDLE-DUM AND TWEEDLE-DEE

TWEEDLE-DUM and Tweedle-dee
Resolved to have a battle,
For Tweedle-dum said Tweedle-dee
Had spoiled his nice new rattle.

Just then flew by a monstrous crow,
As big as a tar-barrel,
Which frightened both the heroes so,
They quite forgot their quarrel.

THREE
BLIND
MICE

THREE blind mice, three blind mice,
   See how they run! See how they
      run!
They all ran after the farmer's wife,
   Who cut off their tails with a carving
      knife,
Did ever you see such a thing in your life
   As three blind mice?

A JAPANESE LULLABY

SLEEP, sleep, on the floor, oh! be good
and slumber;
    For when thou art asleep
    Just hear what I shall do, dear.

Far o'er the mountain will I go and buy thee
    All sorts of pretty toys
    And bring them home to baby.

And when thou early wak'st to-morrow
morning,
    Thou shalt eat red beans
    And fish, my baby.

I HAD A LITTLE DOG

I HAD a little dog, and they called him Buff,
    I sent him to the shop for a ha'porth of
        snuff;
But he lost the bag, and spilt the snuff,
So take that cuff, and that's enough.

A Country Walk

Come, take a country walk with me,
We'll sketch the things that we shall see.

BROW BRINKY

Brow brinky,
Eye winky,
Chin choppy,
Cheek cherry,
Mouth merry.

The first glimpse of the Sea

Count the waves
One, two, three.
One for Paul,
One for Tom,
And one for me.

I SAW A
SHIP
A-SAILING

I saw a ship
      a-sailing,
A-sailing on
      the sea;

And oh! It was all laden
With pretty things for thee!

There were comfits in the cabin,
    And apples in the hold;
      The sails were made of silken stuff
And the masts were
    made
     of
    gold.

DANCE TO YOUR DADDY

DANCE to your daddy,
 My little babby;
Dance to your daddy,
My little lamb.

You shall have a fishy,
In a little dishy;
You shall have a fishy,
When the boat comes in.

KITTY'S KITE

It was a lovely day, and there was a nice breeze blowing, so off went Kitty to the Common to fly her new kite.

On the way she met Teddy.

"Oh, Kit," he said, "is that your new kite? What a beauty. I wish—"

He was going to say, "I wish I had one like it," but he stopped just in time. Kitty was such a kind little girl that she might want to give her kite to him, and that would never do!

"I've just got to go to the shops for mother," said Teddy. "Then I'll come back and help you. May I?"

"Yes, **do**," answered Kitty.

So Teddy ran off, whistling happily.

It was just as he left the Common and was turning off on to a little path that led to the town, that Teddy stumbled over something that lay in his way.

It was a purse—a large, fat purse!

Teddy picked it up and looked inside. It was full of money, or at least, so it seemed to him.

"How I **wish** I could keep it," he sighed, for

Teddy never had very much money.

But he must not do that, he knew, so putting the purse safely in his pocket, he set off for the police station.

He had not gone far when he saw an old lady in the distance. She was stooping down and peering at the path.

Teddy ran to her quickly.

"Have you lost something?" he asked.

"Yes," said the old lady; "my purse. I must have dropped it as I came from the Common. Dear, dear! It had quite a lot of money in it, too!"

"Here it is," said Teddy. "I'm **so**

glad I found it."

The old lady looked at him through her spectacles as she took her purse.

"You are an honest little boy," she said, and, opening the purse, she took out a note and handed it to Teddy.

But Teddy put his hands behind his back.

"No," he said, getting very red, "I couldn't."

"Very well," said the old lady. "Then I am going to buy you a little present. Come along to the shops with me, and if you don't tell me of something you really **want**, I may get quite the wrong thing, you know!"

Teddy could not say "No" this time to the kind old lady, without being rather rude, he thought, and

s o o n
t h e y
w e r e
going
i n t o
Pike's
T o y
Shop
hand-in-hand.

"Oh Teddy," said Kitty, half-an-hour later. "You've got a kite **just** like mine. I **am** glad."

Then Teddy told the story of how he got his kite, and he and Kitty had a lovely time together on the Common.

Pease porridge hot, pease porridge cold,
Pease porridge in the pot, nine days old.
  Some like it hot,
  Some like it cold,
Some like it in the pot, nine
              days old.

A STAR

HIGHER than a house, higher than a tree; O! whatever can it be?

TWINKLE, TWINKLE, LITTLE STAR

TWINKLE, twinkle, little star,
  How I wonder what you are!
Up above the world so high,
Like a diamond in the sky.

When the blazing sun is gone,
When he nothing shines upon,
Then you show your little light,
Twinkle, twinkle, all the night.

Then the traveller in the dark
Thanks you for your little spark.
He could not tell which way to go,
If you did not twinkle so.

A RED SKY IN THE MORNING

A RED sky in the morning
  Is the shepherd's warning,
A red sky at night
Is the shepherd's delight.

LADY MOON

LADY MOON

"LADY Moon, Lady Moon, where are you
    roving?"
       "Over the sea."
"Lady Moon, Lady Moon, whom are you
    loving?"
       "All that love me."

"Are you not tired with rolling, and never
      Resting to sleep?
Why look so pale and so sad, as forever
      Wishing to weep?"

"Ask me not this, little child, if you love me;
      You are too bold.
I must obey my dear Father above me,
      And do as I'm told."

"Lady Moon, Lady Moon, where are you
    roving?"
       "Over the sea."
"Lady Moon, Lady Moon, whom are you
    loving?"
       "All that love me."

LORD HOUGHTON.

MARCH WINDS AND APRIL SHOWERS

MARCH winds
and April
showers

Bring forth May
flowers.

THE PUDDING STRING

SING, sing, what shall I sing?
    The cat has eaten the pudding-string!
Do, do, what shall I do?
    The cat has bitten it
    quite in two.

DINGTY DIDDLETY

DINGTY did-
dlety, my
mammy's maid,
She stole oranges,
  I'm afraid;
Some in her poc-
ket, some in her
  sleeve,
She stole oranges,
  I do believe.

WHEN THE WIND BLOWS

WHEN the wind blows,
  Then the mill goes;
When the wind drops,
Then the mill stops.

LITTLE BOY BLUE

LITTLE Boy Blue, come blow your horn !

The sheep's in the meadow, the cow's in the corn.

Where's the boy that looks after the sheep ?

He's under the hay-cock, fast asleep.

Will you wake him? No, not I ;

For if I do, he'll be sure to cry.

HUMPTY DUMPTY

HUMPTY Dumpty sat on a wall,
Humpty Dumpty had a great fall;
Not all the king's horses, not all the king's men
Could set Humpty Dumpty together again.

HUMPTY DUMPTY.

JACK SPRAT.

SEE-SAW, MARGERY DAW

SEE-SAW, Margery Daw,
    Jack shall have a new master;
And he shall have but a
    penny a day,
Because he can't work
    any faster.

JACK SPRAT

JACK SPRAT could eat no fat,
    His wife could eat no lean;
And so betwixt them both, you see,
    They lick'd the platter clean.

FAM'LY CARES.

WHEN I looked in
  on Baby-girl
    This morning, she
  was sad.
Her " fam'ly " was
    quite seedy,
And a "drefful night" they'd had.

" Poor Joey has a cold " she said.
  " And Sandy has the 'flu,
And Peter has the weasels.*
  Oh, whatever shall I do ? "

* Measles.

IF I HAD A DONKEY

IF I had a donkey and
he wouldn't go,
Do you think I'd
beat him? No,
no, no!
I'd put him in the
stable and give
him some hay,
And say " Gee-up,
Neddy —
away, away,
away!"

CHARLEY WAG

CHARLEY
wag, Charley
wag
Ate the pudding
and left the
bag.

ELSIE MARLEY

ELSIE MARLEY is grown so fine
    She won't get up to feed the swine,
But lies in bed till eight or nine,
And surely she does take her time.

Do you ken Elsie Marley, honey?
The wife who sells the barley, honey?
She won't get up to feed her swine.
And do you ken Elsie Marley, honey?

FRIDAY NIGHT'S DREAM

FRIDAY night's dream
    On the Saturday told
Is sure to come true,
    Be it never so old.

HANDY SPANDY

HANDY Spandy, Jack-a-dandy,
    Loved plum-cake and sugar candy;
He bought some at a grocer's shop,
And out he came hop, hop, hop.

PAT·A·CAKE, PAT·A·CAKE, BAKER'S MAN.

Pat a cake,
Pat a cake,
Baker's man,
Bake me a cake
As fast as you
can.

Pat it and prick it
And mark it
with "B", —
And bake in
the oven for
Baby and
me.

H.G.C.
Marsh
Lambert

THE FAIR MAID WHO THE FIRST OF MAY

GOES to the fields at break of day,
    And washes in dew from the hawthorn tree,
Will ever after handsome be.

OXFORDSHIRE CHILDREN'S MAY SONG

SPRING is coming,
spring is coming,
Birdies, build your
nest;
Weave together straw
and feather,
Doing each your best.

Spring is coming, spring is coming,
Flowers are coming, too:
Pansies, lilies, daffodillies
Now are coming through.

Spring is coming, spring is coming,
All around is fair:
Shimmer and quiver on the river,
Joy is everywhere.

We wish you a happy May.

THE BOYS AND THE BEGGAR.

ONCE upon a time there were two little brothers, named Rollo and Roland. They were twins, and lived in a little hut with their mother, who was very poor, so Rollo and Roland did not often have any money to spend.

But one day a nobleman who was  passing through the forest saw the two boys as they were gathering fire-wood, and he gave them each a silver piece.

As the two children ran home to tell their mother of their good fortune they came on a poor old woman. She seemed to be nearly blind, and was feeling her way along the path with the help of a stick.

Roland brushed past her quickly, but Rollo stopped, and asked her if he could do anything for her.

"Could you spare me a penny?" asked the poor old woman. "I have far to go, and—"

"Of course I can," answered Rollo, gladly, and he pressed his silver piece into the old woman's hand.

"Bless you!" said the other. "Stay

Rollo gives away his silver piece.

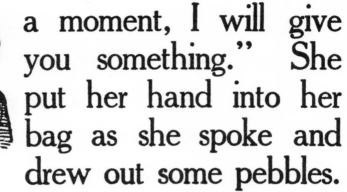 a moment, I will give you something." She put her hand into her bag as she spoke and drew out some pebbles. "Put them in your pocket," she said, and, feeling rather surprised, Rollo did so. Then, after wishing the old dame good-bye, he ran on to his home.

Roland had shown his silver piece to his mother, and now she turned to Rollo and said: "You have had a piece of good fortune to-day, my son!"

But when Rollo confessed that he had given away his silver piece, his mother and brother were quite angry.

"Foolish boy!" cried his mother.

"We are poor enough, as it is, without giving away the little we get to strangers!"

Rollo hung his head, and then he drew out the pebbles which the old woman had given him.

But they had all turned into nuggets of solid gold!

"She must have been a fairy!" gasped Rollo.

Roland gave a cry of surprise. Then, seizing his own silver coin, he dashed out of the hut.

"I will go after the old woman and give

her my silver piece," he said to himself. "Then I shall get nuggets of gold, too."

But as he went, he remembered he had an old and valueless coin.

"I will give that to her instead," he said, "and keep my silver piece."

So when Roland came up to the old woman, he said to her: "Can I do anything for you?" just as his brother had done.

"Can you spare me a penny?" asked the old woman.

"That I will," answered Roland, eagerly, and he handed the false coin to

the old woman, who put it in her bag without looking at it. Then she gave him some pebbles, and told him to put them in his pocket, and without waiting even to say "thank you," Roland ran home with his treasure.

Directly he got to the hut the greedy boy turned his pocket inside out on to the table.

Ugh! What had happened? Out of his pocket there fell nothing save a lot of ugly, crawling little toads—and—the silver piece was gone. It had fallen through a hole in the pocket, and was lost.

OVER THE WATER TO CHARLEY

Over the water and over the sea,
And over the water to Charley.
I'll have none of your nasty beef,

I'll have none of your barley:
But I'll have some of your good oatmeal,
To make an oat cake for my Charley.

The Pet Lamb.

MARY'S LAMB

MARY had a little lamb,
  Its fleece was white as snow;
And everywhere that Mary went
  The lamb was sure to go.

It followed her to school one day:
  That was against the rule;
It made the children laugh and play
  To see a lamb at school.

And so the teacher turned it out,
  But still it lingered near,
And waited patiently about
  Till Mary did appear.

And then it ran to her and laid
  Its head upon her arm,
As if it said, "I'm not afraid—
  You'll keep me from all harm."

"What makes the lamb love Mary so?"
  The eager children cry.
"Why, Mary loves the lamb, you know,
  The teacher did reply.

TEDDY'S ADVENTURE.

I woke up last night when 'twas ever
                                                    so dark
          And the house was all silent and still,
And I thought: "Why, I've left my
                    dear Teddy Bear out
          All alone on the nursery sill!"

So I crept down the stairs,
          and the nursery clock
          Struck one as I opened
                              the door,
And my heart felt a little
          bit thumpy
          As I pit-pattered over
                    the floor.

But when I
looked out of the
window and saw

What was happ'ning, I **did** have
a scare!—
For Teddy Bear wasn't **alone** on
the sill,
A crowd of wee brownies were there!

And they weren't being kind to poor
Teddy at all,
They were dancing all round and about,
And were pulling and punching and
tugging him so
That I thought his poor arms would
come out!

"You've **got** to
come with us, you
silly old thing,
While we dance
in the light of the
moon,

You're lumpy and bumpy and fat,"
they all cried,
"But we'll make you come with us!—"
and soon—

I believe they'd have dragged him
right down from the sill,
And over the grass and away,
But I tapped on the window—
those brownies so brave
Didn't stop to hear what I would say!

But they tumbled right over the top
of the sill
And away they all scurried so fast,
That in less than a second, or it seemed
so to me,
They were gone from the first to
the last !

Then I opened the window and picked
up my bear,
And kissed him on top
of his head,
And I took him upstairs,
and I cuddled him tight,
As I carried him with
me to bed.

OH, DEAR, WHAT CAN THE MATTER BE?

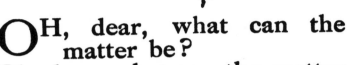

OH, dear, what can the matter be?
Oh, dear, what can the matter be?
Oh, dear, what can the matter be?
Johnny's so long at the Fair!

HERE'S FINIKY HAWKES

HERE'S Finiky Hawkes,
As busy as any,
Will well black your shoes,
And charge but a penny.

THE SAND CASTLE.

Dig in the sand,
Splash in the sea,
Build a great castle –
It's fun for you and me.

THE THREE-LEGGED RACE

Over the sands we run with glee,
Who'll have a three-legged race
with me?

Up goes my
shuttlecock,
ever so high,
It looks like a
baby bird
learning to fly.

BATTLEDORE AND SHUTTLECOCK.

We've paddled and prawned by the
                    dear old Sea;
But now it is time to run home to tea

CURRANTS

HIGGLEDY, piggledy,
 Here we lie,
Picked and plucked
And put in a pie.
My first is snapping,
Snarling, growling;
My second's busy,
Romping and prowling.
Higgledy, piggledy,
Here we lie,
Picked and plucked
And put in a pie.

LAST MONDAY WEEK

Last Monday week it rained so hard
    For nearly all the day,
That Nurse said I must stay indoors
    And not go out to play.

But after tea
(at five o'clock
    I think it was,
    about),
I knelt up by the
window, 'cause

    I wanted to
    look out.

144

And in the gar-
den, just ' below,

I saw the
strangest
sight !

(I suppose you
won't believe it,

But it's true though, honour bright).

There, in a puddle, four wee elves
Were having such a bath !
They dived and splashed
and spluttered so,
I simply **had** to
laugh !

Oh dear! They must have heard me too,
For out they quickly hopped,
And hid behind a laurel bush.
Then, when the rain had stopped

I searched all round, but could not see
A sign of them again,
And ever since last Monday week
I've looked for them in vain.

Baby, baby bunting,
    Daddy's gone a-hunting
To get a little rabbit's skin
    To wrap his Baby Bunting in.

OLD MOTHER GOOSE.

OLD MOTHER GOOSE

OLD Mother Goose,
    When she wanted to wander,
Would ride through the air
    On a very fine gander.

Mother Goose had a house,
    'Twas built in a wood,
Where an owl at the door
    As sentinel stood.

She had a son Jack,
    A plain-looking lad,
He was not very good,
    Nor yet very bad.

She sent him to market,
    A live goose he bought;
"Here, mother," says he,
    "It will not go for nought."

Jack's goose and her gander
    Soon grew very fond,
They'd both eat together
    And swim in one pond.

1, 2, 3, 4, 5, – Catching fishes
all alive,
6, 7, 8, 9, 10, – There! I let them
go again!

BESSY BELL AND MARY GRAY

BESSY Bell and Mary Gray,
    They were two bonny lasses:
They built their house upon the lea,
    And covered it with rashes.

Bessy kept the garden gate,
    And Mary kept the pantry;
Bessy always had to wait,
    While Mary lived in plenty.

GRANNY'S CHAIR

I'm fond of pretty
    silken stuffs,
I'm fond of
    satin too,
And all the lovely
    shimm'ry things
They show in
    shops to you.

But do you know the stuff I love
    Far more than any other?
It is the chintz on Granny's chair
    (She is my Mummy's mother).

It has wee birds and butterflies,
    Big peacocks too are there,
Some little stems of lavender,
    And roses everywhere.

There's lilac and
there's mignonette,
In tiny bunches
on it,
And pretty purple
pansies too
Show (faded
now) upon it.

I know it isn't 'spensive stuff,
It isn't rich or rare——
But there are none quite
like **that** one——
The chintz on
Granny's chair.

SKIPPING

Skippity, slippity, over the rope,
I'll skip to a hundred and over,
I hope!

There was a
    little girl,
And she had a
    little curl
Right in the
    middle of her
        forehead,

When she was
    good,
She was very
    very good,
But when she
    was naughty
    she was horrid!

THERE WAS A LITTLE GIRL.

Hush, Baby, my dolly, I pray you don't cry,
And I'll give you some bread and some milk
  by and by
Or perhaps you like custard?—Or maybe a
  tart?
Then to either you're welcome, with all of
  my heart.

A PATTERN BABY

WHEN people come to call and tell
About their babies, dear me, well—

I sit and listen all the while
And smile myself a little smile.

If mine were like some people's, there,
I would not keep her, I declare!

Their babies scream and cry and fret,
Won't eat or sleep, while my dear pet

She *never* cries; she'll stay for hours
Just looking at the birds and flowers.

The sweetest little cot has she,
All pink and white, as smart can be.

And when at night I lay her in it
She shuts her eyes in half a minute.

That all the babies in the city
Are not like mine I think a pity.

The only thing is, mine won't grow—
She is a baby doll, you know.

E. A. MAYO.

HINK, MINX!

HINK, minx! the old
    witch winks,
  The fat begins to fry.
There's nobody at home but
    jumping Joan,
  Father, mother, and I.

IF I'D AS MUCH MONEY AS I COULD TELL

IF I'd as much money
    as I could tell,
I never would cry
    "Young lambs to sell,
Young lambs to sell,
    young lambs to sell;"
I never would cry,
    "Young lambs to sell."

TOMMY KEPT A CHANDLER'S SHOP

TOMMY kept a chandler's shop;
    Richard went to buy a mop.
Tommy gave him such a whop,
That sent him out of the chandler's shop.

IS IT A, E, I, O, OR U?

Can you fill in the lost vowel?

MSSMLLYHLLSSWRTNGTHSBGBLLNNK

The letters above will make a complete sentence when you have filled in the missing vowel. It is the same one all the way through.

THE LARK

"Bother!" said Betty, crossly, "I don't want to go out this morning; I want to finish this painting-book. Surely Baby might stay in for once!"

But she got up as she spoke, put away her paints, and tied Baby's bonnet on over her curls.

"Come along," she said, "I'll have to take you, I s'pose."

Betty wasn't generally cross like that, and she felt a little ashamed of herself as she and Baby went down the road and turned off into their favourite lane. Here and

there starry primroses were peeping from the hedge, and the pussy-willow was showing its soft, furry, grey buds. Everything looked so peaceful that Betty soon forgot her bad temper, and helped Baby to make a little chain of primroses.

Suddenly a beautiful clear song rose into the air near them.

"I am so hap-hap-hap-hap-happy," it seemed to say, and Betty jumped to her feet and looked up in the sky. Far above her, fluttering his little wings, was a wee brown bird. He was singing away so joyfully that the

whole of his little body seemed to shiver and shake with the strength of his song.

It was the lark.

"How happy he is," said Betty. "He never seems to tire of singing, and yet I s'pose he really works ever so hard. He must have to spend lots of time looking for food for his wife and babies, and yet, directly he gets a spare minute, up-up-up he goes, singing away as if he would never stop! I think" said Betty, "that I'll try to be a little more like him," and, taking Baby's hand, she danced all down the lane with her, singing as she went.

The Lark.

H.G.C.
Marsh
Lambert

My Pigeons . . .

LADY BIRD, LADY BIRD, FLY AWAY HOME

LADY bird, lady bird, fly away home,
    Your house is on fire, your children
      all gone;
All but one, and her name is Ann,
And she crept under the pudding pan.

A SUNSHINY SHOWER

A Sunshiny
    Shower
Won't last
Half an hour.

THE LOST DOLL

I ONCE had a sweet little doll, dears,
  The prettiest doll in the world;
Her cheeks were so red and so white, dears,
  And her hair was so charmingly curled.
But I lost my poor little doll, dears,
  As I played in the heath one day;
And I cried for her more than a week, dears;
  But I never could find where she lay.

I found my poor little doll, dears,
  As I played in the heath one day;
Folks say she is terribly changed, dears,
  For her paint is all washed away,
And her arms trodden off by the cows, dears,
And her hair not the least bit curled;
Yet for old sakes' sake she is still, dears,
The prettiest doll in the world.

CHARLES KINGSLEY.

The Lost Doll.

MY SQUIRREL

There is a squirrel in our
wood,
She's very fond of me,
Because I
often take
some milk
And leave it near her tree.

One afternoon 'twas very hot,
And so I took a book,
And sat just near my squirrel's tree,
In my own shady nook.

And then some horrid boys came by.
They went to climb
the tree,
To rob my little
squirrel's nest,
I couldn't let **that** be.

And so I turned my pockets out,
    And gave them all my money,
To leave my squirrel's nest alone
    They seemed to think it funny.

"Now here's a
riddle, Jill,
for you,
— Why
did the
Owl howl?"

* * * *

"I know! —
Because the
Woodpecker
Would peck 'er,
— horrid fowl!"

H.G.C.
Marsh
Lambert

THERE WAS AN OLD WOMAN TOSS'D UP IN A BASKET

THERE was an old woman toss'd up
    in a basket,
    Ninety times as high as the moon;
Where she was going, I couldn't but ask it,
    For in her hand she carried a broom.

"Old woman, old woman, old woman,
  quoth I,
  "O whither, O whither, O whither so
    high?"
"To brush the cobwebs off the sky!"
  "Shall I go with thee?"
    "Ay, by and by."

BOW, WOW, WOW!

"BOW, wow, wow!"
"Whose dog art thou?"
I am Tom Tinker's dog,

Bow,

  wow,

    wow!"

THE SAMPLER.

Great Grandmamma's sampler is ever
so old,
And it hangs on the dining-room wall;
And among the big pictures it looks
rather sad,
—Rather faded, and yellow, and small.

But I love that old
sampler Great
Grandmamma did.
I love it the best of
them all.

Great Grand-
mamma worked it
when she was a
child,
Just a tiny girl
smaller than me,

THE SAMPLER.

Yet the letters and patterns are beautif'lly
done,
And the stitches are ever so wee
—And I think I can see her, those long
years ago,
With her 'broidery frame on her knee.
I think I can see her, so earnest and
still,
So little and prim and
sedate,
With her plump fingers
flying now
in and now
out,—
(She finish-
ed it when
she was
eight)

—And her head on one side as she
pauses to see
If her stitches are really quite straight.
Great Grandmamma's sampler is ever
so old,
And it hangs on the dining-room wall;
And among the big pictures it looks
rather sad,
—Rather faded, and yellow, and small.
But I love that old sampler, Great
Grandmamma did.
I love it the best of them all!

FINGER-NAILS

CUT them on Monday, you cut them for health;
Cut them on Tuesday, you cut them for wealth;
Cut them on Wednesday, you cut them for news;
Cut them on Thursday, a new pair of shoes;
Cut them on Friday, you cut them for sorrow;
Cut them on Saturday, see your true love to-morrow;
Cut them on Sunday, ill-luck will be with you all the week.

GREGORY GRIGGS

GREGORY GRIGGS, Gregory Griggs,
  Had twenty-seven different wigs.
    He wore them up; he wore them down
To please the people of the town;
He wore them east, he wore them west;
But never could tell which he liked best.

LITTLE BETTY BLUE

LITTLE Betty Blue
  Lost her holiday shoe.
What can little Betty do?
  Why, give her another
  To match the other,
And then she may walk in two.

HUSH-A-BYE, BABY

HUSH-A-BYE, Baby, on the tree top,
  When the wind blows the cradle
    will rock;
When the bough breaks the cradle will
    fall,
Down will come Baby, and cradle, and
    all.

GEORGIE PORGIE

GEORGIE PORGIE, pudding and pie,
  Kiss'd the girls and made them cry;
When the girls came out to play
Georgie Porgie ran away.

LITTLE BETTY BLUE

HUSH·A·BYE·BABY ON THE TREE TOP

I love little pussy, her coat is so warm,
And if I don't hurt her, she'll do me no harm;
So I'll not pull her tail nor drive her away,
But pussy and I very gently will play.

I LOVE LITTLE PUSSY.

LITTLE MISS MUFFET.

LITTLE GIRL, LITTLE GIRL

LITTLE girl, little girl, where have you
been?
Gathering roses to give to the Queen.
Little girl, little girl, what gave she you?
She gave me a diamond as big as my shoe.

LITTLE MISS MUFFET

LITTLE Miss Muffet sat on a tuffet,
Eating her curds and whey;
There came a great spider and sat down
beside her,
And frighten'd Miss Muffet away.

BABY-GIRL'S DREAM.

WHEN Baby-girl wakes up, she comes
    And tells her dreams to me.
And sometimes they are funny.   Then
    I laugh and so does she.
But if they're sad, I say " Cheer up,
    They are not real, you see."

She said this morning that she'd had
    Some simply lovely dreams.

Baby·girl's Dream.

A darling little star
came down
Right in her room,
it seems,
And lighted her and
everything,
With bright and twinkly beams.

The little star said "Do you know,
I've something here for you.
I knew you liked nice dreams, and so
I've brought you one or two.
And here they are, all safely wrapped—
—Now, Baby, dream them, do."

And then he squeezed her hand and
    went,
    But left the dreams behind.
So Baby dreamt them, and they were
    The nicest you could find.
"Dear little star," said Baby-girl,
    "I do think he was kind!"

LITTLE TEE WEE

LITTLE Tee Wee
    Went to sea
In an open boat,
And while afloat
The little boat bended,
▪ ▪ ▪ ▪ ▪ ▪
—And my story's ended!

THERE WAS AN OLD WOMAN LIVED
UNDER A HILL

THERE was an old woman lived under
    a hill;
And if she's not gone, she lives there still.

A CHINESE NURSERY SONG

THE mouse ran up the candlestick,
  To eat the grease from off the wick,
    When he got up, he could not get down,
But squeaked to waken all the town:
  Ma-ma-ma! Ma-ma-ma!

THE BABY OVER THE WAY

"THE Baby over the way, I know,
    Is a better Baby than me;
For the Baby over the way is all
    That a Baby ought to be.

"The Baby over the way is neat,
    When I'm not fit to be seen;
His frock is smooth and his bib is sweet,
    And his ears are always clean.

"He's wide awake when he's put to bed,
    But *he* never screams nor cries;
He lies as still as a mouse, 'tis said,
    And closes his beautiful eyes.

"*He* never wanted a comforter,
    Nor sips of tea from a spoon;
He never crumpled his pinafore,
    He never cried for the moon.

"He's a dear little, sweet little angel bright,
A love and a dove, they say;
But when I grow up, I am going to fight
With the Baby over the way!"
                              FAY INCHFAWN.

DAVY, DAVY DUMPLING

DAVY, Davy Dumpling,
    Boil him in the pot;
Sugar him and butter him,
    And eat him while he's hot.

IF ALL THE WORLD WAS APPLE-PIE

IF all the world was apple-pie,
   And all the sea was ink,
And all the trees were bread and cheese,
What should we have to drink?
It's enough to make an old man
Scratch his head and think.

POP GOES THE WEASEL

HALF a pound
   of tuppeny
   rice,
   Half a pound of
   treacle;
That's the way the
   money goes—
Pop goes the
   weasel!

THE MOON MAN.

I dreamt the
   Moon Man
said "If you
   Will come, my
   little dear,
And keep house for me, you shall live
   On jam and ginger beer.
I love you so." The Moon Man sighed,
   (I thanked him much, and bowed.)
" So won't you travel back with me
   Upon this fleecy cloud?"
I said I would, and up we went
   Until we reached the Moon.
But oh! I longed for home again

So very, very soon,
Because the tale he'd
told to me
Was anything but
true.
I found I had to cook
and clean,
And do the washing too!
And when my day was over with
The grease and grime and dirt,
I had to sew the buttons on
That horrid Moon Man's
shirt.
Or else I had to light
a fire
(With flint and
tinder box)

Or find his boots and spectacles,
  Or darn his hole-y socks.

And as for what he'd said about
  My jam and ginger-beer,—
I never saw them once! Nor did
  He call me " little dear."
He fed me on the stalest crusts

Of bread that
he could find,
And when there
was a piece of
cheese,
He only gave
me rind.

At last I struck.
    I said to him,
" I simply will not
        stay !—
I'm going in a minute now
    When I have had my say.
You'll have to cook your
        dinners and
    To turn your
        puddings out,
And if you won't,
    'tis very clear
You'll have to
    do without ! "

He made a dreadful face at me.
  He took me by the hair.
I screamed and screamed. He let me go,
  And I fell through the air—
Down—down—till with a gentle bump
  I landed on my head—
And woke. Where was I? I was safe
  Inside my cosy bed!

Daisy Chains

MARY, MARY, QUITE CONTRARY

MARY, Mary, quite contrary,
   How does your garden grow?
With cockle shells and silver bells
   And cowslips all in a row.

GOOSEY, GOOSEY, GANDER

GOOSEY, goosey, gander, where shall
   I wander?
Upstairs and downstairs, and in my
   lady's chamber.

There I met an old man
who would not say his
prayers,
I took him by the left leg
and threw him down
the stairs.

POOR GERALDINE

My nurse had tucked
        me up in bed
And put the curtains
        right,
And shut the door
        behind her, with
    "Now pleasant dreams. Sleep tight!"

But oh! I simply **couldn't** sleep
    That lovely starry night.

I watched the little fleecy clouds
    Go softly sailing by,
I watched the little silver stars
    A-twinkling in the sky;
But still I **couldn't** go to sleep—
    I lay and wondered why.

And as a distant nightingale
    Sang softly with a trill—

I saw there
was a
fairy
there
Upon my
window-
sill!

I didn't move a teeny bit,
But lay so quiet and still.

And then she fluttered softly in,
And very, very soon
I saw her fly (there
was, you know,
A lovely shining
moon)
To where my dolly
Geraldine
Had slept all after-
noon.

She still was there, and
  as I watched,
    I saw that
fairy go
And take
      her own wee garment off,
  And then—and then—d'you know
She took my dolly's frock instead!
How could she treat her so?

      I called aloud:
          "Oh, fairy dear,
    I **am** ashamed of you!"
    She waved her hand to
          me and then
    An airy kiss she blew,
    And laughed a little
          tinkling laugh,
    And through the win-
          dow flew!

I didn't think that fairies could
  Behave so, I'll confess!
I went to Geraldine and found
  Just by her—can you guess?—
A little 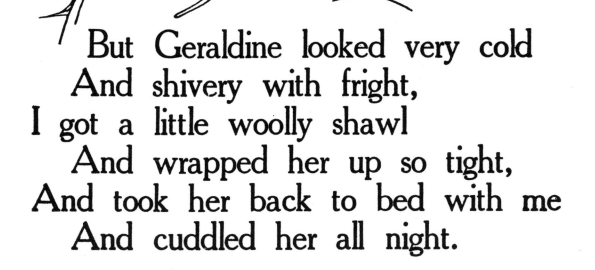 pile of cobwebs there,
  It was the fairy's dress!

  But Geraldine looked very cold
  And shivery with fright,
I got a little woolly shawl
  And wrapped her up so tight,
And took her back to bed with me
  And cuddled her all night.

And all the next day I was just
  As busy as could be,
For Geraldine had got to have
  Some other clothes, you see;
And now I let her sleep at night
  Quite safe in bed with **me.**

WHEN JACKY'S A VERY GOOD BOY

WHEN Jacky's a very good boy,
    He shall have cakes and a custard;
But when he does nothing but cry,
    He shall have nothing but mustard.

LITTLE BOB SNOOKS

LITTLE Bob Snooks was fond of his **books**,
    And loved by his usher and master.
But naughty Jack Spry, he got a black **eye**,
    And **carries** his nose in a plaster.

LUCY LOCKET lost her pocket;
Kitty Fisher found it;
There was not a penny in it,
But a ribbon round it.

LUCY LOCKET LOST HER POCKET.
KITTY FISHER FOUND IT.

FAIRY TEA-CUPS

Baby Bunting was strolling down the garden path where the Canterbury bells grew. They were white ones—the kind that look like dear little cups inside wee saucers. Baby Bunting loved them.

But this afternoon Baby Bunting suddenly stood still and gave a little whistle of surprise.

The plants looked different ! Lots of the dear little flowers were gone, and only the stalks remained.

"Oh-h-h !" said Baby Bunting.

"Somebody's been pulling off our tea-cup flowers—I—"

Hark! Surely that was the sound of voices?

Baby Bunting peered behind a clump of tall flowers which grew near. Beyond them was a little square patch of grass, and—right in the middle of the grass—what **do** you think was going on?

A fairy tea-party!

There could be no doubt about it!

In the middle of the group sat the Fairy Queen,

 with a little gold crown on her head, and all round her were gathered her ladies - in - waiting, while busy little elves ran to and fro, carrying plates made of rose petals, on which rested the most delicious little cakes you ever saw. Piles of sugared violets and cherries were arranged on leafy dishes, and as the fairies helped themselves to the good things they talked and laughed merrily.

But what surprised Baby Bunting most of all was to see their tea-cups. They were the little white Canterbury bell flowers that were missing from the plants. **Now** these flowers

were standing in a row on the grass, and a busy elfin butler was filling them to the brim with honey dew.

"Well!" gasped Baby Bunting, staring in surprise, "I **didn't** think fairies would do such a thing! To take our flowers and——"

But at the first sound of a human voice the fairies scattered right and left. Off went the elves with the plates and dishes, the ladies-in-waiting gathered up the Fairy Queen's train, and before Baby Bunting could reach the spot every one of them had disappeared. Only the Canterbury bell flowers remained!

"THE LADIES-IN-WAITING GATHERED UP THE FAIRY
QUEEN'S TRAIN."

"I'm sorry I frightened them so," said Baby Bunting, gathering up the little white flowers, "but I **do** think the fairies ought to have asked if they might use our tea-cups!"

．　．　．　．　．

In a few days a lot more flowers had come out on the Canterbury bell plants, and they looked as pretty as ever. But the fairies never took any more of them to use as tea-cups. I expect they were ashamed to, don't you?

THE QUEEN OF HEARTS

THE Queen of Hearts
   She made some tarts,
All on a summer's day;

The Knave of Hearts
He stole the tarts,
And with them ran away.

The King of Hearts
Called for the tarts,
And beat the Knave full sore;

The Knave of Hearts
Brought back the tarts,
And said he'd ne'er steal more.

There was a little man and he wooed a little maid,
  And he said, "Little maid, will you wed, wed, wed? —
I have little more to say than will you — yea or nay? —
  For least said is soonest mend-ded-ded-ded!"

The little maid replied, (some say a little sighed)
  "But what shall we have for to eat, eat, eat?
Will the love that you're so rich in make a fire in the kitchen?
  —Or the little god of love turn the spit, spit, spit?"

OLD CRADLE SONG

SLEEP, baby, sleep!
Thy father guards
the sheep,
Thy mother shakes
the dreamland
tree,
And from it fall
sweet dreams for
thee.
Sleep, baby, sleep!
Sleep, baby, sleep!

RAIN, RAIN, GO AWAY

RAIN, rain, go away,
Come again
another day;
Little Mary wants to
play.

I HAD A LITTLE NUT TREE

I had a little nut tree,
  nothing would it bear,

Save a silver nutmeg
  and a golden pear.

The King of Spain's
  daughter came to
  visit me

And all for the sake
  of my little nut
  tree.

GO TO BED FIRST

Go to bed first, a golden purse;
  Go to bed second, a golden pheasant;
Go to bed third, a golden bird.

GREEDY NED.

Such a
Greedy young scapegrace
is Ned,
Currant buns send him right
off his head!
One day for his tea,
He consumed
twenty three,
And has since been
confined to his
bed.

Ride, ride, little
 Baby shall ride,
And have a wee
 puppy-dog
  tied to her side.
—And a wee
 pussy-cat
  tied to the
   other, —

And away
 she shall ride
To see her
 Grandmother.

ROUND AND ROUND

Round and round the garden
Like a teddy bear;
One step, two step,
Tickle you under there.

GLOVES.

As I was going o'er London Bridge,
I met a cart full of fingers and thumbs!

IF "IFS" AND "ANS"

If "ifs" and "ans"
Were pots and pans,
There'd be no need for
tinkers!

Thomas Tipp.
Tinker.

THE ROCK-A-BYE LADY.

SHEILA was coming home through the cornfield. On either side of her grew the beautiful golden wheat, with here and there a moon daisy or a poppy peeping out from behind the corn-stalks. She stopped to look at an extra fine poppy.

"Take me home with you," said the poppy, softly.

Sheila jumped. "Did—did you speak?" she asked.

"Yes," answered the poppy.

"The corn is going to be cut to-morrow, and the poppies will all be cut down with it. It's such a pity, because lots of us are still only in bud, you know."

"You've got three buds yourself," said Sheila, looking closely at the little plant.

"I know," answered the poppy. "That's why I asked you to take me home with you. If you'd break off my stalk close to the ground you would get all my buds as well, and in water they would come out and show you their pretty red petals. I'm nearly over, of course—"

"I'd love to take you home with me," said Sheila, and she carefully broke off the plant close to the ground as she spoke.

"Thank you," said the poppy gratefully. "I won't forget that you've been kind to me, and to-night, when my petals fall, you shall have a lovely dream."

So Sheila took the poppy home with her, buds and all, and stood it in water in her bedroom. Then she told her big sister Irene all about it.

Irene was grown-up,

and Sheila was rather afraid she might laugh and say that her little sister had imagined it all. But she didn't. She listened ever so interestedly, and then said, "I wish it had happened to me, Sheila. It reminds me of those verses of Eugene Field's :—

" The Rock-a-bye Lady from
       Hushaby Street
Comes stealing ; comes creeping ;
The poppies they hang from her
       head to her feet—
And each hath a dream that is
       tiny and fleet—
She bringeth
her poppies to
you, my sweet,
When she
findeth you
sleeping !..."

"I think the poppy that spoke to you must be the one belonging to the Rock-a-bye Lady, don't you, Sheila?"

"I wonder," said Sheila.

.   .   .   .

She went to bed early that night, and as she undressed, Sheila noticed that the petals of the poppy had all fallen off.

"Now for my lovely dream," she said to herself, as she curled up in bed, and in another minute she was fast asleep.

And what a nice dream she had, too! She dreamt that she had wandered

away and away to a far-off, wonderful land, where the Rock-a-bye Lady lived, and where all the nice dreams are made. She played hide and seek with the fairies, and helped them to wrap up the dreams in the Rock-a-bye Lady's poppies all ready for her to take to earth and give away to the babies and tiny children.

Then she went for a ride on a Moon-beam, too, and paid a visit to the Cloud Elves, and drank real dew out of a crystal goblet, and helped the stars to play peek-a-boo. It was all such lovely fun, and Sheila was ever so sorry to wake up at last and find herself in her own little bed, with the sunshine pouring in at the window.

TO BED, TO BED

"TO bed, to bed," says Sleepy-head;
 "Let's stay awhile," says Slow;
"Put the pot on," says Greedy John,
 "We'll sup before we go."

LITTLE TOM TUCKER

LITTLE Tom Tucker, sing for your supper.
 What shall he sing for? White bread
  and butter.
How shall he cut it without any knife?
How shall he marry without any wife?

The Wind

When the
wind is in
the North,
The skilful
fisher goes
not forth,

When the
wind is
in the
East
'Tis neither
good for
man
nor
beast,

When the
wind is in
the South,
It blows the
bait in the
fishes'
mouth,—

But when the
wind is in
the West,—
Then 'tis at
its very best!

THE ROBIN

WHEN father takes his spade
    to dig
Then Robin comes along;
He sits upon a little twig
And sings a little song.

Or, if the trees are rather far,
He does not stay alone,
But comes up close to where we
    are
And bobs up on a
    stone.

LAURENCE ALMA-TADEMA.

The North Wind doth blow and we shall have snow,
And what will the robin do then — poor thing?
He'll sit in a barn and keep himself warm,
And hide his head under his wing — poor thing!

Feeding the Dicky-birds.

PIT, PAT, WELL-A-DAY

PIT, pat, well-a-day,
   Little Robin flew
      away.
Where can little Robin
   be?
Gone into the cherry
   tree.

LITTLE LAD, LITTLE LAD

LITTLE lad, little lad,
   Where wast thou
      born?
Far off, in Lancashire,
   Under a thorn,
Where they sup sour
   milk
In a ram's horn.

COBBLER, COBBLER, MEND MY SHOE

COBBLER, cobbler, mend
my shoe:
Get it done by half-past two;
Do it neat, and do it strong.
I will pay you
when it's
done.

AS I WENT TO BONNER

AS I went to
Bonner,
I met a pig with-
out a wig.
Upon my word
and honour.

BARBER, BARBER, SHAVE A PIG

BARBER, barber, shave a pig,
    How many hairs will make **a wig**?
"Four-and-twenty, that's enough."
Give the barber a pinch of snuff.

A THORN

I WENT to the wood and got it,
    I sat me down and looked at it,
The more I looked at it, the less I liked it,
And brought it home because I couldn't
    help it.

THE SNOWMAN

Making a Snowman is ever such fun.
Don't you think ours is a fine big one?

ANN

THERE was a girl in our towne,
Silk an' satin was her gowne,
Silk an' satin, gold an' velvet,
Guess her name:
—three times I'ye tell'd it.

NOW CHRISTMAS IS COME

NOW Christmas is come
Let us beat up the drum,
And call all our neigh-
bours together;
And when they appear
Let us make them
such cheer
As will keep out the
wind and the weather.

THE CHRISTMAS TREE.

Down to the duck pond, and
over the ice —
Skating in Winter is ever so nice!

TOM, TOM, THE PIPER'S SON

TOM, Tom, the piper's son,
   Learnt to play when he was young,
But the only tune that he could play
Was "Over the hills and far away";
Over the hills, and a great way off,
And the wind will blow my top-knot off.

Now Tom with his pipe made such a noise,
That he pleased both the girls and boys,
And they stopped to hear him play
"Over the hills and far away."

Tom on his pipe did play with such skill,
That those who heard him could never
   keep still;

Whenever they heard they began for to
  dance—
Even pigs on their hind legs would after
  him prance.

As Dolly was milking her cow one day,
Tom took out his pipe and began for to
  play;
So Doll and the cow danced "the Cheshire
  round,"
Till the pail was broke, and the milk ran on
  the ground.

———

I HAD A LITTLE HOBBY-HORSE

I HAD a little hobby-horse,
  And it was dapple grey.
Its head was made of pea-straw;
  Its tail was made of hay.

I sold it to an old woman
  For a copper groat;
And I'll not sing my song again
  Without a new coat.

THE SQUIRREL

THE SQUIRREL

THE winds they did blow,
  The leaves they did wag;
Along came a beggar-boy,
  And put me in his bag.

He took me up to London:
  A lady did me buy;
Put me in a silver cage,
  And hung me up on high.

With apples by the fire,
  And nuts for to crack:
Besides a little feather-bed
  To rest my little
    back.

WILLY BOY, WILLY BOY

WILLY boy, Willy boy, where are you
    going?
  I'll go with you, if I may.
I'm going to the meadow to see them a-
    mowing,
  I'm going to see them make hay.

SPINNING TOPS

Crack! Goes the little whip,
        Spin! Goes the top—
Looking as though it meant
             Never to stop

BABY BUNTING'S "FAM'LY"

When Baby Bunting goes to bed,
  The "Fam'ly" must go too,
And when you call to say "Good-night,"
  They all get shown to you.

     They're made of plush and
               furry cloth,
     And mostly stuffed with bran.
     And Peter is the best beloved
      He **is** a dear wee man.

(He's really Peter Rabbit,
        though,
     With tiny shirt of blue,
And Mummy's had to patch
        him where
His knees were coming through.)

Then next him is a "Chickie"
  With beak and eyes so green,

The very strangest chicken that
I think I've ever seen.
Joey and 'Possum next to
                          him,
And then a dear grey
                    Bunny.

Chickie

(Young Joey is a
                monkey small,
And 'Possum's
            very funny)
His nose is snub, his
                  tail is fat,

'Possum

Joey.

And—well—I must confess,
That just **what** little 'Possum is
No one can ever guess!

And next comes cuddly
                    Teddy bear,

Bunny.

And then no less than five
Dear doggies in a little row,
    All looking quite alive!

"Here's Bobby, Sandy,
            Paddy, Pip,"
    Will Baby Bunting say,
And Timothy–who's like the dog
    That b'longs to Auntie May."

So then you kiss them, one and all,
    And Baby says, "That's right."
And when you've tucked the blankets 'n
    You wish them all "Good-night."